Elite Warriors

JULIA GARSTECKI

BLACK RABBIT BOOKS

Bolt is published by Black Rabbit Books
P.O. Box 3263, Mankato, Minnesota, 56002.
www.blackrabbitbooks.com

Marysa Storm, editor; Grant Gould & Michael Sellner, designers; Omay Ayres, photo researcher

Library of Congress Cataloging-in-Publication Data
Names: Garstecki, Julia, author.
Title: SEALs / by Julia Garstecki.
Description: Mankato, Minnesota : Black Rabbit Books, [2019] | Series: Bolt. Elite warriors | Includes bibliographical references and index. | Audience: Grades 4-6. | Audience: Ages 9-12.
Identifiers: LCCN 2017024432 (print) | LCCN 2017025880 (ebook) | ISBN 9781680725469 (ebook) | ISBN 9781680724301 (library binding) | ISBN 9781680727241 (paperback)
Subjects: LCSH: United States. Navy. SEALs–Juvenile literature. | United States. Navy–Commando troops–Juvenile literature.
Classification: LCC VG87 (ebook) | LCC VG87 .G37 2018 (print) | DDC 359.9/84–dc23
LC record available at https://lccn.loc.gov/2017024432

Printed in China. 3/18

Image Credits

Alamy: AF archive, 4–5, 6; Stocktrek Images, Inc., 5 (choppers), 9 (top), 27, 28–29; americanspecialops.com: US Navy/Photographer's Mate 1st Class Arlo K. Abrahamson, 20; commons.wikimedia.org: Mitch Barrie, 16 (rifle); Rama, 16 (pistol); US Air Force/Master Sgt. Jeffrey Allen, 25; US Navy/John Sullivan, 9 (bttm); US Navy/Mass Communication Specialist 2nd Class Kyle D. Gahlau, 21 (bttm); US Navy/Petty Officer 3rd Class Blake R. Midnight, 24; US Navy/Sanandros, 23; US Navy/Shane T. McCoy, 22 (left), 22 (right); US Navy/Slick-o-bot, 32; commons.wikimedia.org/sealswcc.com: US Navy, 16 (top); Dreamstime: Oleg Zabielin, Cover; navy.mil: US Navy, 10; US Navy/Chief Photographer's Mate Andrew McKaskle, 18–19; navy.mil/commons.wikimedia.org: US Navy/Senior Chief Mass Communication Specialist Andrew McKaskle, 13; navytimes.com: US Navy/MC1 Lawrence Davis, 21 (top); Shutterstock: BLACKDAY, 14–15 (bkgd); FabrikaSimf, 31; Getmilitaryphotos, 3; Tony El-Azzi, 16 (knife); VanderWolf Images, 1
Every effort has been made to contact copyright holders for material reproduced in this book. Any omissions will be rectified in subsequent printings if notice is given to the publisher.

CONTENTS

CHAPTER 1

In ACTION

On a moonless night, two helicopters fly to the country Pakistan. They carry a team of Navy SEALs. The choppers fly toward a building. One of the United States' most wanted criminals is hiding inside.

The soldiers plan to sneak inside the building. But the **mission** goes wrong. One of the choppers hits the building. The element of surprise is gone. But the SEALs know just what to do.

Mission Accomplished

Working together, the SEALs fight their way inside the building. They climb a staircase and find their target. They shoot. They kill. The soldiers then board choppers. They fly out of Pakistan. The mission is complete.

Who Are the Navy SEALs?

Navy SEALs are highly trained U.S. soldiers. They are called in to stop dangerous enemies. They sneak into enemy territory to gather information. When a job seems impossible, SEALs jump to action.

The first two SEAL teams officially formed in 1962. Over time, more teams developed. Now, many SEAL teams perform missions around the world.

The name SEAL comes from where the soldiers work. It stands for sea, air, and land.

How Many SEALs? (as of May 2017)
322,390
total active duty
Navy personnel
about
2,500
SEALs

CHAPTER 2

Many Jobs, MANY PLACES

SEALs perform many different jobs. They work in all kinds of environments too. SEALs have fought enemies in mountains. They've rescued **hostages** at sea.

Getting to these places can be difficult. Sometimes SEALs arrive by parachute. The soldiers also travel by chopper, submarine, and boat.

Underwater Missions

SEALs often work underwater. Soldiers map **harbors** and seas. They gather information to help plan larger missions. SEALs can even attach mines to ships.

SEALs are sometimes called frogmen. The nickname comes from how much time the soldiers spend in water.

WHERE SEALs HAVE WORKED

SEALs have worked in many places. On some missions, they gathered information. Other times, they fought enemies. Here are a few of their missions.

Grenada
1983
rescued Grenada's governor

Panama
1989
captured Panama's dictator

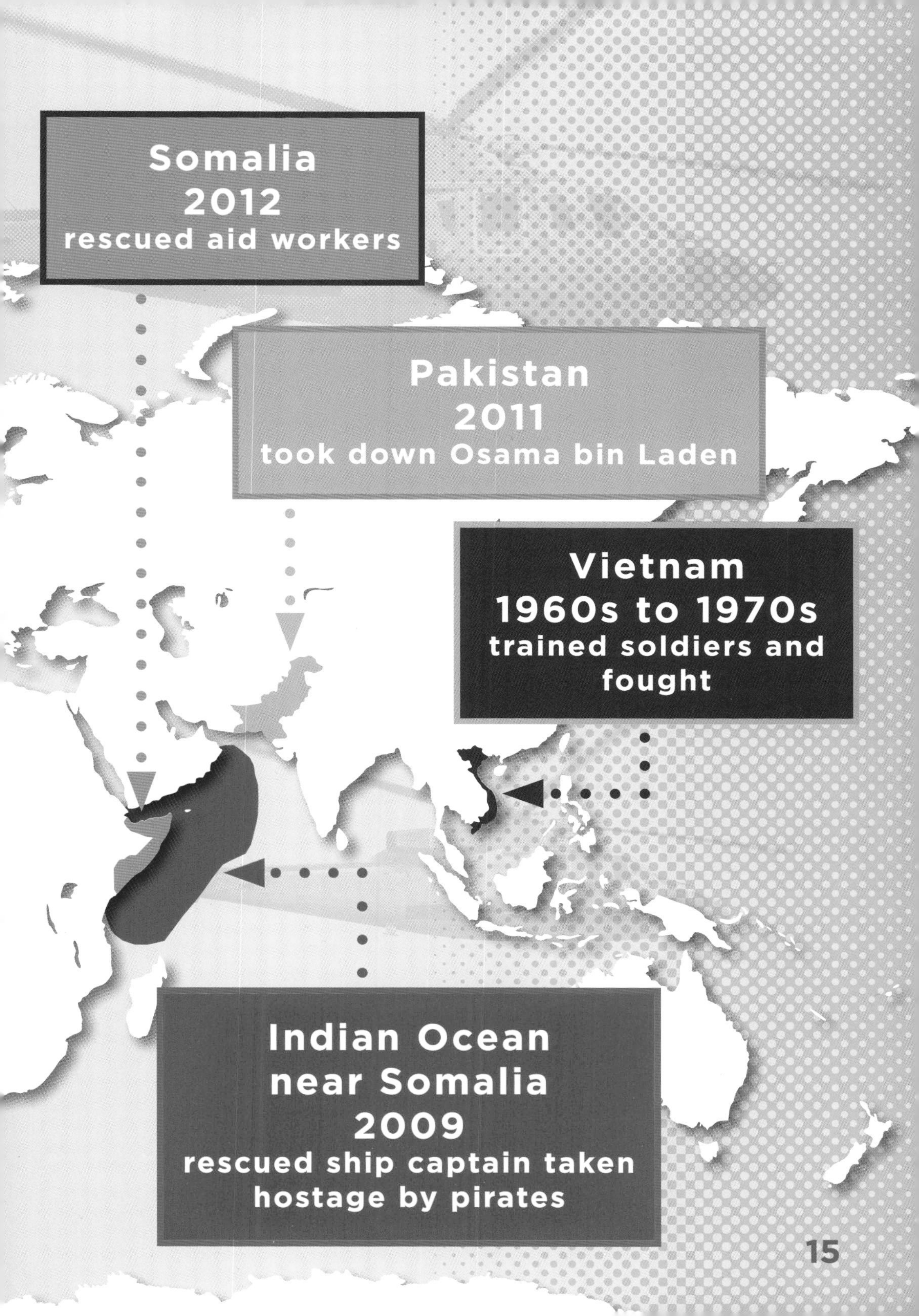

Somalia
2012
rescued aid workers

Pakistan
2011
took down Osama bin Laden

Vietnam
1960s to 1970s
trained soldiers and fought

Indian Ocean
near Somalia
2009
rescued ship captain taken hostage by pirates

SEAL Weapons
rifle
pistol
knife

CHAPTER 3

WEAPONS and Gear

SEALs use many kinds of weapons. Their gear depends on the mission. Most soldiers carry a rifle and pistol. They may use climbing or diving equipment. They might need explosives to enter buildings. SEALs also use high-tech vehicles.

SEAL DELIVERY VEHICLE (SDV)

SEAL delivery teams use minisubs. They help soldiers travel underwater.

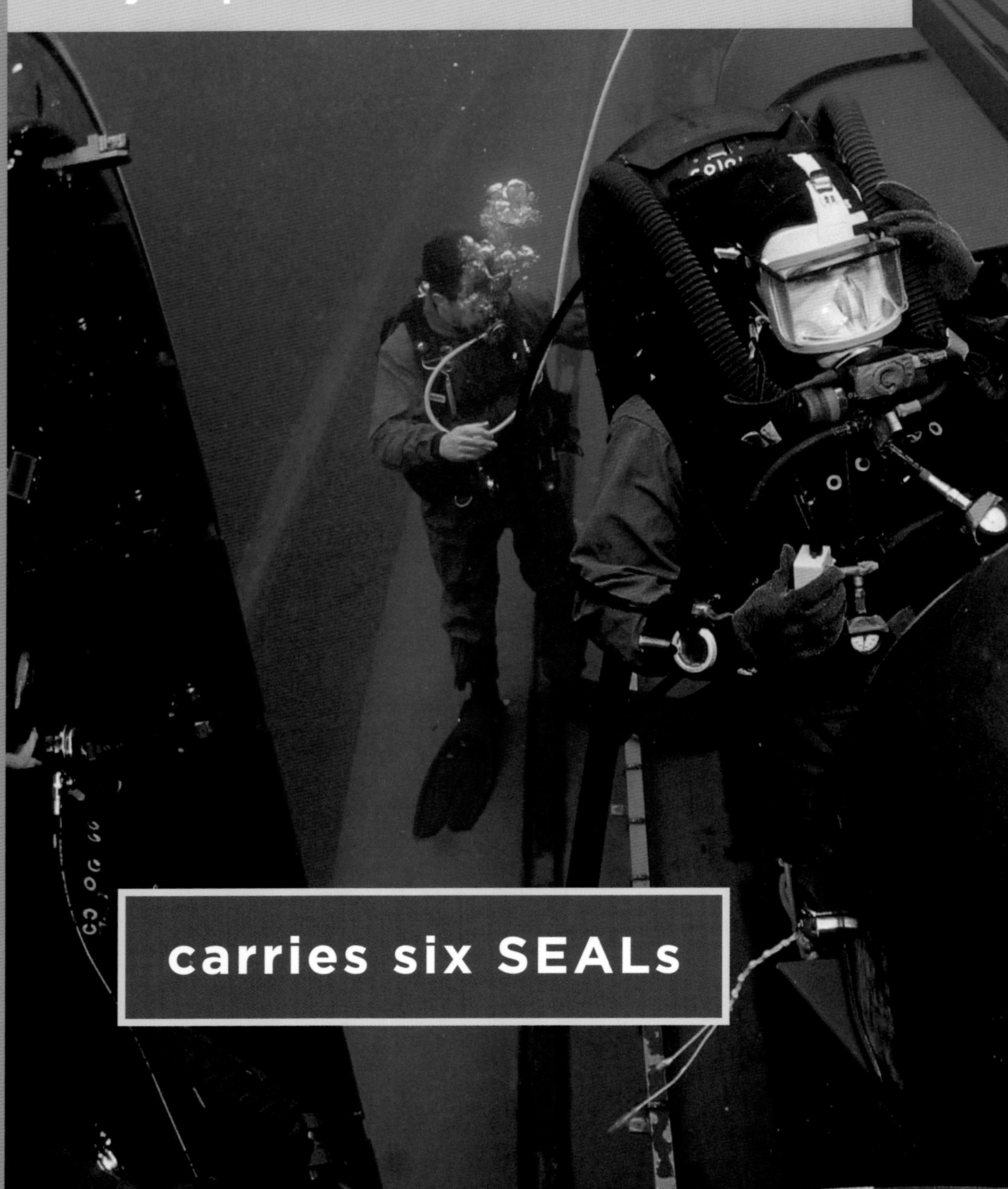

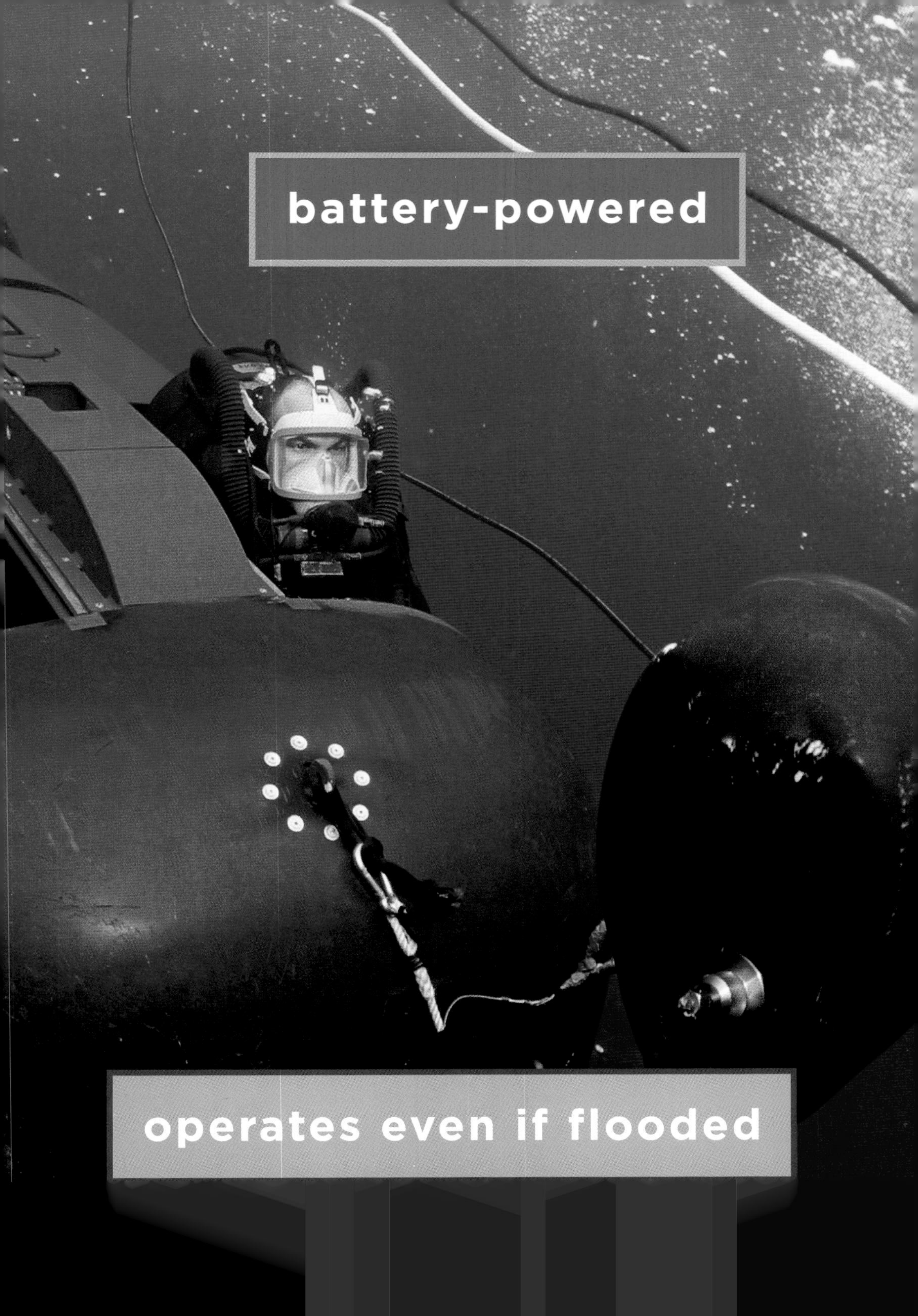

battery-powered

operates even if flooded

CHAPTER 4

TOUGH Training

Becoming a SEAL isn't easy. **Recruits** must go through brutal training. It can last more than 30 months. A large part of training is Basic Underwater Demolition/ SEAL training (BUD/S). Soldiers train for hours every day. They must be mentally tough too.

The Three Phases of BUD/S

THIRD PHASE
land warfare training

Hell Week

BY THE NUMBERS

HOW FAR RECRUITS RUN

MORE THAN
200
MILES
(322 KILOMETERS)

One part of BUD/S is called Hell Week. During the week, recruits train nearly nonstop. They work in **harsh** conditions.

5½ days
LENGTH

ABOUT 4 HOURS
TOTAL AMOUNT OF SLEEP RECRUITS GET

more than

20 HOURS

HOW LONG RECRUITS TRAIN EACH DAY

75

PERCENT OF SOLDIERS WHO DROP OUT DURING HELL WEEK

SEALs work in the air. Recruits must also go through parachute training.

In the Sea and Sky

On some missions, SEALs must swim long distances. They often carry heavy gear at the same time. Recruits do many exercises during BUD/S to prepare. They must swim with their hands and legs tied together. They exercise while carrying heavy logs.

Super Skills

During training, SEALs learn many skills. They learn how to **navigate** and make maps. They also work with explosives and practice first aid. A SEAL must be ready for anything.

Always Prepared

SEALs are the best of the best. They train for days or months before a job. It doesn't matter where they're sent. These elite warriors are always ready.

GLOSSARY

dictator (DIK-tey-ter)—a person who rules with total power and often in a cruel way

harbor (HAHR-ber)—a part of a body of water that is next to land, protected, and deep enough to provide safety for ships

harsh (HAHRSH)—severe or cruel

hostage (HAHS-tij)—a person captured by someone else

mission (MISH-uhn)—a job assigned to a soldier

navigate (NAV-i-geyt)—to find the way to get to a place when you are traveling

pistol (PIS-tl)—a small gun whose chamber is part of the barrel

recruit (ri-KROOT)—a newcomer to a group or field of activity

rifle (RI-ful)—a shoulder weapon with grooves in the barrel

BOOKS

Bozzo, Linda. *Navy SEALs.* Serving in the Military. Mankato, MN: Amicus High Interest, an imprint of Amicus, 2015.

Slater, Lee. *Navy SEALs.* Minneapolis: ABDO Publishing Company, 2016.

Whiting, Jim. *Navy SEALs.* U.S. Special Forces. Mankato, MN: Creative Education, 2015.

WEBSITES

How the Navy SEALs Work
science.howstuffworks.com/navy-seal3.htm

Join the Elite Community of US Navy SEALs
www.navy.com/careers/special-operations/seals.html#ft-key-responsibilities

Navy SEALs
navyseals.com

INDEX